MACAROONED
ON A DESSERT
ISLAND

MACAROONED
ON A DESSERT
ISLAND

BY JOHNETTE DOWNING
ILLUSTRATED BY
CHRISTINA WALD

To Coco
Eat It Up!

PELICAN PUBLISHING COMPANY
GRETNA 2014

To Antoinette de Alteriis–J. D.

For the much-maligned broccoli, in all of its delicious forms–C. W.

*The word "Pelican" and the depiction of a pelican are
trademarks of Pelican Publishing Company, Inc., and are
registered in the U.S. Patent and Trademark Office.*

Library of Congress Cataloging-in-Publication Data

Downing, Johnette.
  Macarooned on a dessert island / by Johnette Downing ; illustrated by Christina Wald.
    pages cm
  Summary: "A dream takes a child to a dessert island, with lollipop trees and a piece of cake for a
bed. Natural snacks abound too: fruits, nuts, and vegetables. Ends with an easy recipe for a healthy
treat"— Provided by publisher.
    ISBN 978-1-4556-1936-8 (hardcover : alk. paper) — ISBN 978-1-4556-1937-5 (e-book) [1.
Stories in rhyme. 2. Desserts—Fiction.] I. Wald, Christina, illustrator. II. Title.
  PZ8.3.D75397Mac 2014
  [E]—dc23
                                                                          2014000156

Printed in Malaysia
Published by Pelican Publishing Company, Inc.
1000 Burmaster Street, Gretna, Louisiana 70053

Being macarooned on a dessert island is
such a treat for me.
Adrift from home, I arrive by sea.

My gingerbread house on cookie land
is near the beach of sugar sand.

By the waves, I draw and doodle.
My beach blanket is made of strudel.

My garden is lined with cupcake flowers
that bloom after gumdrop showers.

I climb granola mountains to view the ocean
and cover up with coconut sunscreen lotion.

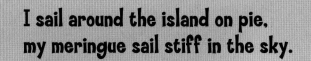

I sail around the island on pie,
my meringue sail stiff in the sky.

The clouds are made of cotton candy.
They make the marmalade sun look dandy.

The key-lime water laps the shore
and a cinnamon campfire toasts my s'more.

A forest of lollipop trees
is where animal crackers roam in the breeze.

Cold rivers of ice cream flow
where banana and cherry trees grow.

Down the rapids I like to float.
Five dozen brownies serve as my boat.

I hike through rock candy careful of my footing.
On peppermint paths, one can slip on pudding.

Once I thought I saw a goose,
but nay—it was vanilla mousse.

I happily spend my time
crafting confections that taste sublime.

I stir and mix and blend all day
making parfait and crème brûlée.

I cook custard, cobbler, and a tart.
You see, I am a baker deep in my heart.

Natural snacks abound.
My daily meals come from the ground.

Apples, oranges, mangos, and pears
grow near melons here and there.

Strawberries and blueberries fulfill my wish
to top the yogurt in my dish.

Pecans and walnuts add some crunch.
Almonds are my favorite. I eat a bunch!

Vegetables are a healthy treat.
Asparagus stalks grow thirty feet.

Broccoli grows as large as trees,
and turnip tops tickle my knees.

I till the garden with my spade
while sweet peas are on parade.

Candied yams tempt my tummy.
Carrot cake for dessert—how yummy!

I dice zucchini for lettuce wraps.
With greens to munch, I don't need naps!

On my dessert island I run and play
until a chocolate sky ends the day.

A piece of cake is my bed
with a marshmallow pillow for my head.

The stars twinkle cones of flavored ice.
My whipped cream blanket feels quite nice.

At night a moon pie shines above
as I drift back home to the people I love.

Oops! To the sink I rush—
after daydreams of sweets, I'd better brush!

We snuggle in bed and read a book.
When I grow up, I'll be a cook.

EASY BREEZY
BERRY BLAST

Serves 1

1 cherry

1 tsp. crushed nuts (almonds, walnuts, and/or pecans)

1 tbsp. whipped cream

1/2 cup mixed berries

1/4 cup plain or vanilla yogurt

Directions

1. Place berries in a colander in the kitchen sink. Rinse the berries with water.
2. Place the yogurt in a serving bowl.
3. Sprinkle berries on top of the yogurt.
4. Top the berries with whipped cream, nuts, and a cherry.
5. Enjoy!
6. Clean your dishes. Every good cook keeps a clean kitchen!
7. Oops! To the sink you must rush—after a sweet treat, you'd better brush!

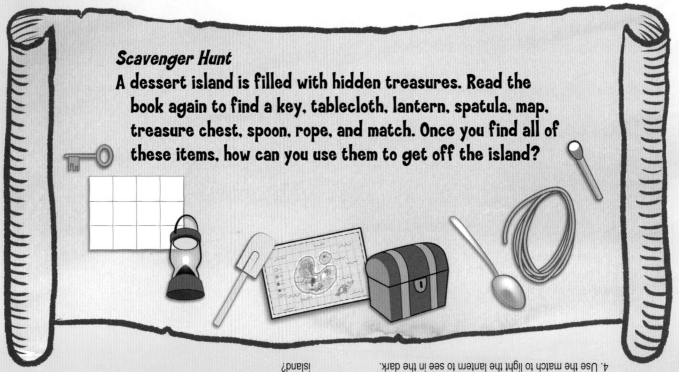

Scavenger Hunt
A dessert island is filled with hidden treasures. Read the book again to find a key, tablecloth, lantern, spatula, map, treasure chest, spoon, rope, and match. Once you find all of these items, how can you use them to get off the island?

Answer: Here is one way to get off the island:
1. Use the key to open the treasure chest. Sit inside to make a boat.
2. Use the rope to tie the spoon to the chest to make a mast.
3. Tie the tablecloth to the mast to make a sail.
4. Use the match to light the lantern to see in the dark.
5. Use the spatula as an oar to paddle the boat away from shore.
6. Use the map to find your way home.

What are some other ways you can use the items to get off the island?